Time Together, Time Well Spent!

Casey Rislov

Illustration by Stephen Adams

AuthorHouse™
1663 Liberty Drive
Bloomington, IN 47403
www.authorhouse.com
Phone: 1-800-839-8640

First published by AuthorHouse 02/23/2015

ISBN: 978-1-4670-4191-1 (sc)
978-1-4817-1497-6 (e)

Library of Congress Control Number: 2011917854

Print information available on the last page.

This book is printed on acid-free paper.

authorHOUSE®

In honor of my Mother who taught me
the love of books from an early age

You make the popcorn;
I'll put in a movie.
We'll sit together
Huddled in one big blanket!

Don't fall asleep;
There's too much action!
Running, chasing,
Snoring, sleeping ...

Don't give up!
There are more points to be made!
Gather, shuffle,
Pass them out!

Dancing, dancing,
Around and around,
All throughout
Our living room—

Laughing, smiling,
Twirling, shaking.
You pick the music;
I'll find the beat!

We can be silly—
There's no end in sight!
Tap, tap, tap,
Move, shake, spin!

Let's read books
Then swap stories.
Mine takes me to
A faraway land.

Dragons, princesses,
Warriors, and kings—
Each has a fate.
What could it be?

Life on the edge,
Life in a castle,
Life spent traveling,
Life made magical.

Let's play ball,
You and me.
I can catch;
You can throw.

Maybe you'll kick it,
Maybe you'll swing.
Keep me guessing,
But please don't go!

Fort! Fort!
Let's build a fort!
I'll get the chairs;
You find the sheets.

Lights off,
Flashlights on.
You make shadow figures.
I'll tell a story.

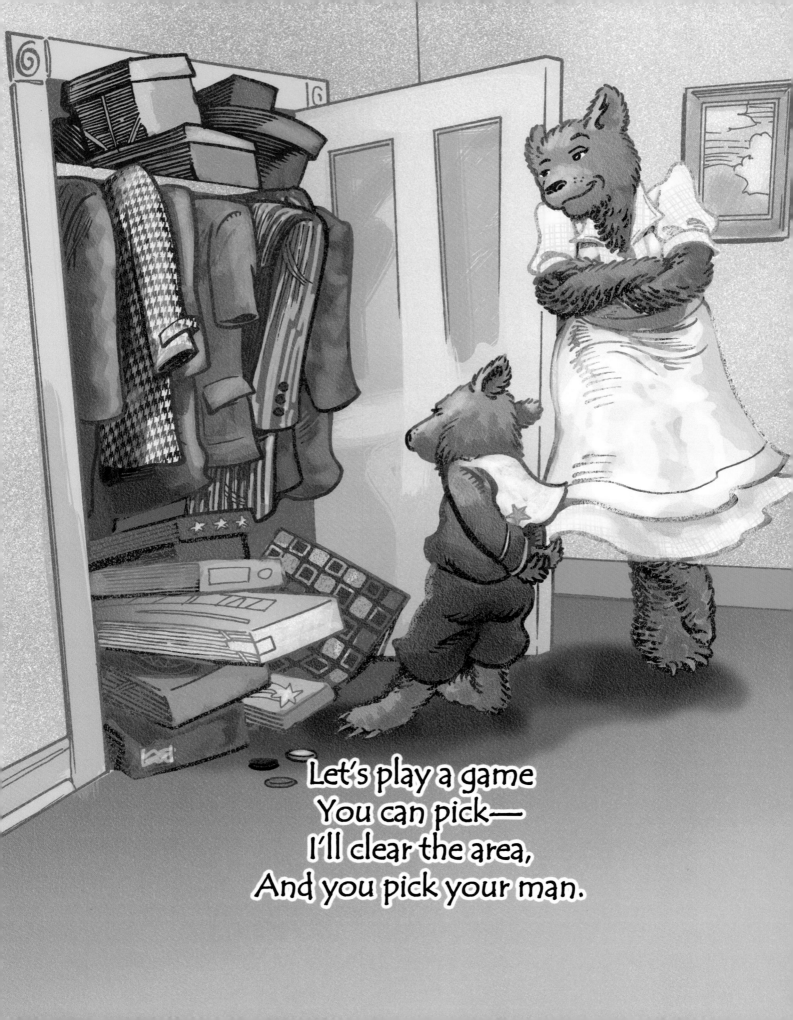

Let's play a game
You can pick—
I'll clear the area,
And you pick your man.

Shaking, rolling—
There go the dice!
I went four,
Now you go five!

This game is close;
This game is tight.
Don't give up
Without a fight!

Time together,
Time well spent!
Time to know you,
Time to do it again!

CPSIA information can be obtained
at www.ICGtesting.com
Printed in the USA
LVIC04n1636041116
511692LV00001B/1

* 9 7 8 1 4 6 7 0 4 1 9 1 1 *